THIS SIDE
TANGLEWOODS
THE AWETHUNDER SCHOOL FOR FAMILIARS
PRANCETOWN
Witch Sideways' house
First Terrestrial Witches' Bank
BANK
The Blue Moon Comfrey Rooms
BLUE MOON
CRAFTY WITCHES CO-OP
BROOM-STICK SALE
HORIZON LINE
TO THE OTHERSIDE
D0810070

17 JUN 2014
SHN

Unwilling MY WITCH skates on thin ice

Hiawyn Oram • Sarah Warburton

30130 149688573

Essex County
Council Libraries

A SHORT HISTORY OF HOW YOU COME TO BE READING MY VERY PRIVATE DIARIES

In a snail shell, they were STOLEN. Oh yes, no less. My witch Haggy Aggy (HA for short) sneaked into my log basket and helped herself.

According to her, this is what happened:

On one of her many shopping trips to Your Side she met a Book Wiz. (I am told you call them publishers, though Wiz seems more fitting as they make books appear, as if by magic, every day of the week.)

Anyway, this Book Wiz/publisher wanted HA to write an account of HER life as a witch here on Our Side. Of course, HA wasn't willing to do that. Being the most unwilling witch in witchdom, she is far too busy shopping, watching telly, not cackling, being anything BUT a witch and getting me into trouble with the High Hags* as a result.

The Book Wiz begged on her knees (apparently) and offered HA a life's supply of shoes if she came up with something. So HA did. She came up with THIS – MY DIARIES. ALL OF THEM!!!!

Of course, when I wrote the diaries, I was not expecting anyone to read them. Let alone Othersiders like you. But as you are, here is a word to the wise about how things work between us:

* The High Hags run everything round here. They RULE.

1. We are here on THIS SIDE and you are there on the OTHER SIDE.

2. Between us is the HORIZON LINE.

3. You don't see we're here, on This Side, living our lives, because for you the HORIZON LINE is always a day away. You can walk for a thousand moons (or more for all I know), but you'll never reach it.

4. On the other paw, we know you're there because we visit you all the time. This is partly because of broomsticks. A broomstick has no trouble with any Horizon Line anywhere. A broomstick (with one or more of us upon it) just flies straight through.

And it has to be like that because scaring Otherside children into their wits is part of witches' work. In fact it is Number One on the Witches' Charter of Good Practice (see copy glued at the back).

On the other paw, it is NOWHERE in the Charter for a witch to go over to Your Side to make friends and try to be and do everything you are and do – as my witch Haggy Aggy does.

But then, that's my giant problem: being cat to a witch who doesn't want to be one. And as you will see from these diaries, it makes my life a right BAG OF HEDGEHOGS. So all I can say is, if HA tries to make friends with YOU, send her straight back to This Side with a spider in her ear.

Thank you,

Rumblewick Spellwacker Mortimer B. xxx

This Diary Belongs to:

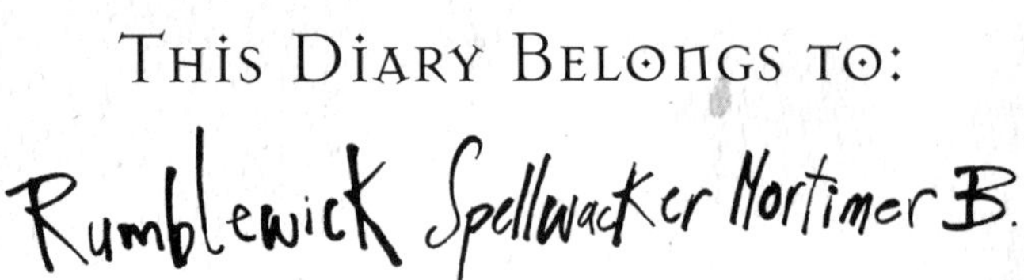

RUMBLEWICK for short, RB for shortest

Address:

Thirteen Chimneys,
Wizton-under-Wold, This Side
Bird's Eye View: 331 N by WW

Telephone:

77+3-5+1-7

Nearest Otherside Telephone:

Ditch and Candleberry Bush Street,
N by SE Over the Horizon

Birth Day:

Windy Day 23rd Magogary

Education:
The Awethunder School For Familiars
12-Moon Apprenticeship to the
High Hag Witch Trixie Fiddlestick

Qualifications:
Certified Witch's Familiar

Current Employment:
Seven-year contract with Witch Hagatha Agatha,
Haggy Aggy for short, HA for shortest

Hobbies:
Catnastics, Point-to-Point Shrewing, Languages

Next of Kin:
Uncle Sherbet (retired Witch's Familiar)
Mouldy Old Cottage,
Flying Teapot Street,
Prancetown

Wake the Dead
Festival

First Night Of Waking The Dead Day

Dear Diary,

Yesterday HA was laughed at and anyone who knows about HA, knows this:

NEVER LAUGH AT HER.

It makes her determined to be so above being laughed at, she wouldn't care if she was hanging from the evening star by worn out boot laces.

Let me explain.

Tonight is the first night of our Wake the Dead Festival. As it involves a lot of dancing – on stony Otherside graves – all the witches go to the Crafty Witches' Co-op and get themselves new dancing boots.

All the witches except Haggy Aggy.

Apparently, she won't be 'seen dead' in Co-op dancing boots.

"Why not?" she snapped when I asked her why not. "Because they're all DEAD boring. So DEAD boring only the DEAD would think of wearing them as they can't be made further DEAD by wearing such DEAD boring boots."

Well, I didn't think I had time in all my lives for such a dead argument and agreed to take her shopping at Stairrods on the Other Side for a pair of completely not dead-boring boots.

We crossed the Horizon Line and immediately met two cross winds. To avoid getting caught up in their quarrel, I braked, reversed and dropped down well below their raging – and that's when HA saw what would lead to her being laughed at.

"Stop, RB!" she yelled. "Take us in to land. We have to see this close up and urgently at hand."

With behindsight I realise it would have been better if I'd taken our chances with the furious winds. But I hadn't and now did what I'm supposed to do. I obeyed my witch's whim and word – and brought us down in the higher branches of a tall tree near what she so urgently wished to ogle.

It was, what seemed to me, a frozen-over boglet, its solid ice giving off a wispy mist. On the ice were Othersiders of all ages, shapes and sizes, gliding, turning, circling, running, dancing – and here's the thing, Diary – they were doing it on

KNIFE BLADES!!!

While HA gasped and clasped and unclasped her hands – as she does when her 'horizon expands' and she gets excited – I made my observations.

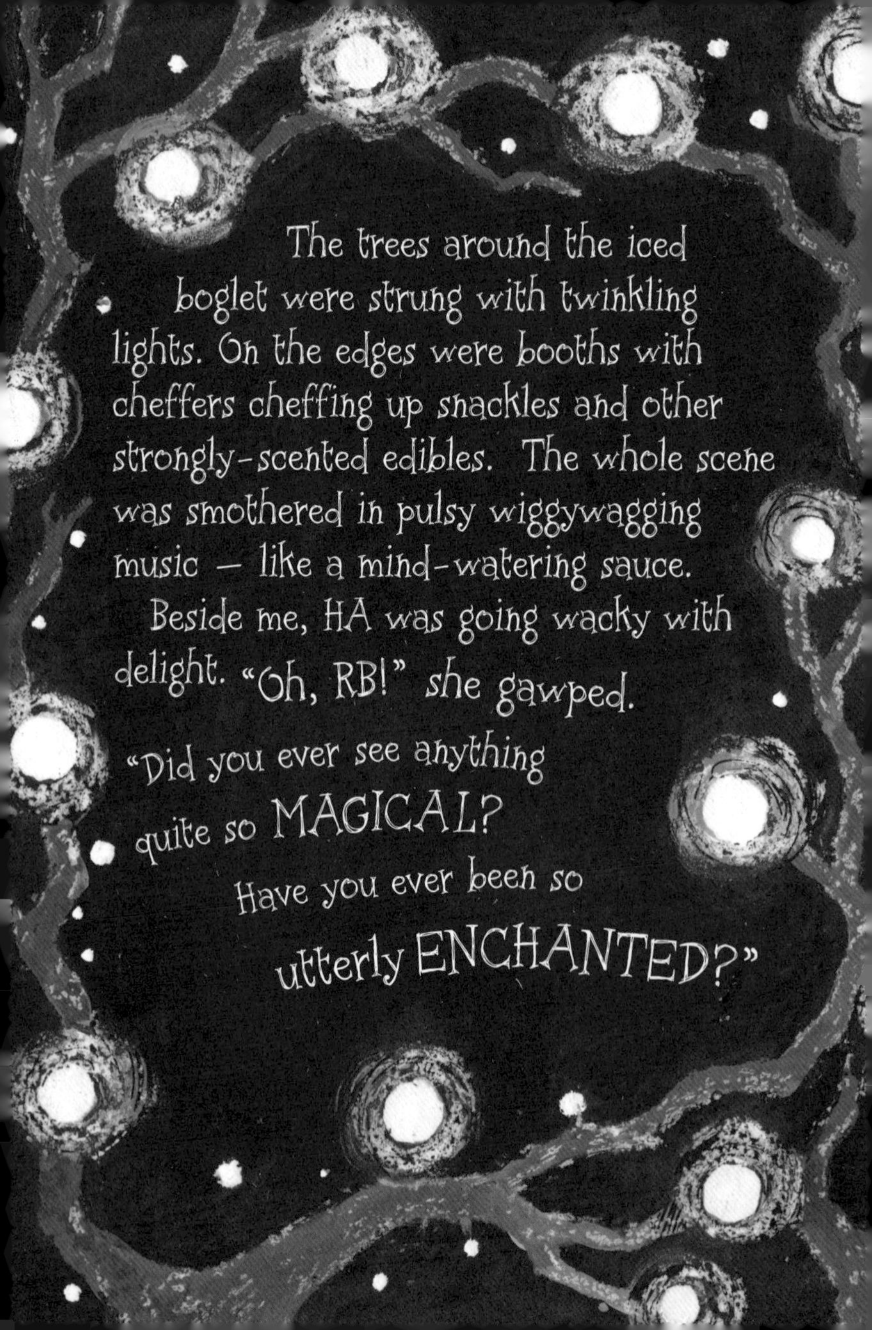
The trees around the iced boglet were strung with twinkling lights. On the edges were booths with cheffers cheffing up snackles and other strongly-scented edibles. The whole scene was smothered in pulsy wiggywagging music – like a mind-watering sauce.
Beside me, HA was going wacky with delight. "Oh, RB!" she gawped.
"Did you ever see anything quite so MAGICAL?
Have you ever been so utterly ENCHANTED?"

Whether I had or hadn't, it didn't matter.

I knew from her tone, we were only one tiny tadpole of a step away from her joining in.

She quickly discovered they were selling the knife blades (set into boots and called skates) at a shop on the edge of the frozen boglet called a rink – together with everything else Othersiders might like to wear while frozen bog dancing.

HA being HA, she was soon blade-booted, scarfed and muffed – and without taking two blinks of an eye to think about HOW – was hurling herself onto that ice.

And IMMEDIATELY fell

FLAT ON HER FACE.

That's when the laughter began. Not great guffaws. Just that thing Othersiders do: snickwittering behind hands while trying to look as if they aren't.

Then someone made the mistake of trying to help her up. Little did they know. HA does not like TO BE SEEN needing help.

She likes to be seen as able to do EVERYTHING perfectly herself.

So she pushed away the helpful Outsider, struggled back onto her blades – and immediately fell flat on her face again.

And the more she couldn't get up, without falling, the crosser she got and the less chance there was she'd let anyone assist her.

And now the laughter wasn't behind hands.

It was out-in-the-open guffawing.

I couldn't stand by doing nothing so I performed the Tried and Trusted 'Your Witch Be Upright' spell:

Oh witch of mine who's fallen
And can no balance keep
Let not your limbs be jumbled
Into a tangled heap,
You are, because I spell you to,
Upon the count of nine
Completely upright standing
And walking upright fine.

It worked and she was walking back to me, admittedly a small distance above the ice – which made everyone gasp – but nevertheless,

NO LONGER FLAT ON HER FACE,

and that's all that mattered. Mind you, she still wasn't ready to give up!!

She nudged a Girl eating a snackle at a brazier. "Tell me, what's the magic for this? I'll swap with you. Isn't that what you call it? Swapping? You give me the Upright-On-Ice spell and I'll give you my Fake-Prince-To-Fat-Pumpkin spell."

The Girl seemed surprised and dropped her snackle but as a Grown came to grab her away, she did call back: "There is no magic. No spell. Just get yourself a good Skating Instructor – and PRACTISE!"

YIKES. Better hide you, Diary – HA's up and calling for her skates!

Later

Dear Diary,

Dashing out but just HAD TO TELL YOU.

At breakfast, HA ordered me to

FREEZE OVER THE DRAGON'S BOG
UNDER WITCH WOOD,
BEYOND THE NARROW AVOID.

And to find her a Skating Instructor at once as advised by that snackle-eating ratlet – so she can 'learn to skate without magic' and 'practise' until she can go back and show those Othersiders who guffawed at her yesterday!!

I tried to put her off, of course. "Forget them. They don't know what you CAN do. And anyway it's nearly time to go Waking the Dead and we still haven't got you new boots."

"Oh, fooey to boots, RB!"
she pouted.
"Fooey to dancing on graves!
What folliculous Dark Ages folderol.
I'd rather go skating. Now go make me that
personal practice rink,
there's a faithful Familiar."

"But what about the Dragon?" I argued. "How will he feel about his playground being frozen over!"

"Just tell him it's for me," she said. "Me, the only witch in witchdom who won't let her Familiar join in Make Dragon's Cry Day, or steal dragons' tears for the purposes of her own selfish spell-making."

"As I remember it," I said, "it wasn't long ago you wanted him slain because his snoring kept you awake at night."

"That was then," she sighed. "And I didn't MEAN it. I only said it to test out a prince I met. To see if he would slay a dragon for me, which he wouldn't because he was a fake. Now please, RB, get to it. And stop wasting tell."

What choice do I have? None. So I'm off to the library to see if I can dig up a bog-freezing spell. What I'll do about an instant Instructor has not yet revealed itself through the mists of my unknowing. And, as I'm not convinced it ever will, all I can say is SOCKS.

Back From The Dragon's Bog

Dear Diary,

I'm home and I've done it. The Dragon's bog is now frozen solid. Though not without incident along the way.

Arriving at the library, I was met by Anchovette on librarian's duty.

Anchovette is Familiar to the High Hag Witch Clover Froggspittal. And I'm sorry to have to put this down in my own writing but it is the truth. Anchovette is sweet on me.

She has that look when she looks at me. It is a very dangerous look – a Quagmire Ahead Look that makes you go YIKES AND DOUBLE YIKES inside because it says as clear as clear moonlight: I would like to start a long line of future familiars with you.

Imagine then, how my heart sank, when I saw her sitting there behind the desk. Imagine the YIKES going on inside me when, with That Look in her eyes, she said, "Can I be of any assistance, dear Familiar Rumblewick?"

Imagine the TRIPLE YIKES, when I shook my head and she took a different direction with her treacle...
"Oh and by the way, it is my expectation that you will dance with me on at least every other grave tonight at Waking the Dead."

Luckily, at that moment I saw my best friend Grimey across the library. With a kind of throat-stuck promise to Anchovette that of course I would dance with her, I hurried over to him and – in whispers that exclude everyone especially librarians – I told him my problems.

He was aghast. "Freeze over the Dragon's bog to make her a personal practice skating rink and find an Instructor to teach her. That's a tall order even for you, RB."

"Tell me about it," I said.

Together we went digging through the library and eventually came with up a Bog Freezing Type spell in a dusty volume called

SPELLS FOR OCCASIONS
SO FAR UNIMAGINED

(so far unimagined, in fact, the seal hadn't yet been broken and we were the first to open the book!!).

Then we moved on to the matter of an Instructor. And agreed it was an impossible task as we were sure no inhabitant of This Side had ever thought of trying to stay upright on knives let alone dance on them.

As we huddled and whispered, Anchovette kept looking over and smirking and doing a bit of her own kind of snickwittering. I found it disturbing.

It was as if she was UP TO SOMETHING that put her ABOVE us...

put her
IN
CONTROL.

After a while, it made me so uncomfortable I decided to remove myself from that library, even if we hadn't answered the question of where to find HA a Skating Instructor.

As I was about to go, Grimey stopped me and whispered very low, "Oh, by the way, RB, you remember my cousin, Claudine? You met her with me in Prancetown. You said you thought she was enchanting. Well, she's hoping to dance with you tonight!"

Well, of course I remembered Claudine! No Quagmire Ahead Look in her eyes. Just enchantment. And now hoping I'd dance with her!!!

My heart took up its own broomstick and did a few fancy moves in a clear night sky it suddenly owned.

As I passed Anchovette, she called, "See you on the first grave! My Hag and I will be expecting you!"

My heart on its broomstick braked because – at the words 'my Hag' – there

WAS her Hag,

Clover Froggspittal,

MATERIALISING

from the air under the desk!!

Out came her pointing finger with its blood moon-coloured talon. Under my chin it went, scratching cruelly.

"Oh yes..." she cackled.

"Very expectant we are, Familiar Rumblewick.

Disappoint our expectations

and be sorry."

Even so, once out of the library, with Froggspittal's cackle fading, I was soon flying again – Claudine in my eyes, speeding me on my way.

First I went to the Co-Op – hardly noticing the battle for last minute boots going on there – and buychased a sprinkling vial and the essential ingredient of the Freezing spell: three stirring spoons of cumulous cloud.

Behind the Co-op, I made up the spell's admixture and set off to cross the Narrow Avoid – haunted as it is by giant bats and alien wizards and Hags Who Can Never Die – thoughts of Claudine banishing my usual dread.

Arriving at the Bog, I drew the Dragon from his cave by throwing balls of bog mud in until he came out. And, eventually – after some lengthy negotiation – got him to agree to the freeze-over provided it was for no more than three moons and strictly for HA's personal use.

And what do you know?

Here IS Haggy Aggy, back from somewhere – probably shopping for skating wear – and yelling the house down for me. Will have to go. Meanwhile, here's that Freezing spell.

SPELL TO FREEZE OVER THE HOT AND FIERY, THE BOILING, THE BUBBLING, THE SQUELCHY, THE SINKING AND THE SULPHUROUS

Fill a clean sprinkling vial with three stirring spoons of cumulus cloud (the fresher the better) and seven of your own deepest breaths. Shake well. On your broomstick, circle that which is to be frozen three times, sprinkling the admixture and chanting:

Cold what isn't, cold will be
Frozen through for all to see
Smooth to touch and white as bone
Hard and cold as rock and stone
No more living, breathing squelch
No more sour and sulphurous belch
For in this charming tad of trice
What wasn't, is now solid ICE!

SMALL PRINT: Use with due care. The effects last three moons and no known spell exists to reverse them sooner.

Dawn Next Day

Dear Diary,

Can you believe this?

I missed the First Night of Waking the Dead!

The <u>whole</u> of it.

When HA came in yelling last night, she had been shopping for skating wear. She wanted to know how she looked in it – though before I could say a word, she told me:

"Fabulous! Utterly fantabulous!! Now all I need is a few instructions, a little practice and I'll show those Otherside Guffawers. Is my rink ready, RB? Is my Instructor instructed to instruct? Of course – because you never let me down. So let's go, let's fly!"

I was almost speechless. There was no way we could get to her 'rink' and back before dawn, which would mean missing the entire first night of Waking the Dead. And given Anchovette's and Froggspittal's expectations and Claudine's hopes that was unthinkable.

WE HAD TO BE THERE.

But HA was having none of it.

"Dancing on graves? Waking the exhausted Otherside dead? When I could be learning to glide on ice like Othersiders under the twinkling stars. Who in their right minds would choose the former?"

"WITCHES!"

I yelled (desperate).

"ALL WITCHES EXCEPT YOU!

And if we aren't there, the High Hags – ONE IN PARTICULAR – will be

WANTING

TO KNOW

WHY!"

"Rubble!" she said. "Witches and their Familiars are coming in from everywhere. There'll be so many, not even the Hags will notice if little old us are there or not."

"But I haven't found you an Instructor," I argued (more desperate). "And I never will because there isn't such a thing ANYWHERE on This Side."

"You'll find one, RB," she said. "I know you. Meanwhile, I'll just have to teach myself. Now, let's go."

"No," I yelled, at the complete end of my patience. "YOU go skating. I'LL go grave-dancing."

"Don't be folderolical!" she laughed. "You haven't got me an *Instructor*, so you'll have to be on hand at all moments to spell me upright when I'm flat on my face."

So skating we went and grave dancing we didn't.

I'll go on when I can. Right now I need to get the fire going. And prepare myself for Froggspittal and Anchovette demanding an explanation for my failure to live up to their frightening expectations.

Later – Back At The Iced Bog

Dear Diary,

Wonders will never cease: *I'm sitting* on the edges of the frozen bog, snug beside a fire, nibbling hot snackles while I scribble –

and happy, dear Diary,

HAPPY!

Outside his cave, watching the proceedings, is an only slightly grumpy Dragon.

Froggspittal – with or without Anchovette – did not come round, festering and pointing her pointing finger.

Biggest wonder of all: Over on the ice HA is being taught to '*swizzle*', 'fishtail' and 'scull' (all skating terms) by a complete and ready-made Skating Instructor named Glidia Glissando!!!

Yes. No sooner had I lit the fire for the breakfast cauldron cakes this morning, there came – not a Hag-type hammering – but a gentle tap on the door.

Into Thirteen Chimneys glid the said Witch, Glidia Glissando. And blow me down with a feather, she introduced herself as a

fully-qualified SKATING INSTRUCTOR

who trains the legendary Skating Witches of Glass in their famous Glassindia Ice Show!!

I admit to being surprised. (How did she know we needed an Instructor? Had Grimey told her?) At the same time, I was so OVER THE MOON with relief, I didn't press her on the details.

And I still am over the moon. Not only does she skate like she was born with bladed boots on, she is also a GREAT teacher.

She and HA are getting on so well, they're cackling like crawbirds together out there on the ice.

I mean. I ask you. When did HA last have a friend with whom she could cackle (music to my ears), glide arm in arm, and 'shoot-the-duck' (another skating term) while having nice witchy chats?

NEVER,

if you ask me.

So, yes, this is as good a morning as I've had in moons. My witch is happy. I'm happy, as I can see no reason why I shouldn't get to Wake the Dead tonight and deliver on both A's expectations and C's hopes.

Oh, and look who comes to make my happiness complete. It's Grimey, flying fast, as if he's afraid I'll eat all the snackles before he gets here!

Later After Grimey Has Gone

Dear Diary,

DISASTER, CATASTER, CRISASTER.

That's what we're facing, Diary.

Grimey didn't come to eat hot snackles with me. He came to impart disastrous news – with three scratches on his nose to prove it!

I asked how he got them.

"I'll tell you. But first I should warn you." He stole a look round at HA and Glidia and lowered his voice. "Your witch is skating on thin ice, RB. Very thin ice.

And so are you."

"What are you talking about?" I said. "That ice is rock solid. I spelled it so myself. And in case you haven't noticed, I'm not skating on anything. I'm sitting here talking to you!"

"I don't mean it as actual fact," he glared. "I say it to describe your situation.

To sum it up.
You're both skating on such thin ice,
it's going to crack
and you'll be up to your necks
in a very sulphurous
bog!

Let me make it clear. These scratches? Anchovette gave them to me last night at grave-dancing. This one for me introducing you to Claudine. This one for you – as you weren't there to get it yourself – for thinking Claudine enchanting. And this one she aimed at Claudine, only I got between them in time."

"Claudine!" I gasped, "how does Anchovette know about her?"

"I'm sorry to tell you, RB," he said.

"She had one of the library's resident eavesdroppers listening in on us!

As soon as you'd gone, I saw the little telltaler drop from his thread. He'd been hanging against a spell book of his own colouring – no doubt why I hadn't spotted him before.

"I watched as he scuttled across the library to report back to Anchovette!

He must have told her everything – especially about Claudine – because soon she was ranting, not caring who heard.

"'I'll teach him,' she raved, 'to find another Familiar enchanting. I'll get my Hag onto him. For assisting his witch in her unnatural longings to ice-dance like Othersiders! I'll have her struck off the Witches' Register and him smoked over a boiling cauldron and sent back, hairless, to kittengarden!'"

"At this, Froggspittal materialised again from somewhere. 'Oh yes, my pet, my treacletart,' she crowed. 'I'll be onto him, don't you fester yourself about that!'"

Grimey stole another look at HA and Glidia and continued.

"They mean badly by you, RB. And the question I have to ask is this. Where did that Skating Instructor come from?"

I told him she had just appeared at our door.

"My point exactly. There is every reason to suspect she's Froggspittal, spelled into the guise of this Glidia Glissando."

"But she can't be!" I stammered. "Glidia trains the Skating Witches of Glass!"

"Does she, indeed," sighed Grimey. "Ever heard of them? I certainly haven't."

"You mean," I breathed.

"THIS IS A TRAP?"

Grimey nodded. "I'm *sure* of it. Trap HA preferring to dance on ice than on graves and they've trapped you for assisting her – as in freezing this bog and finding her an *Instructor*. Don't you see? It's Anchovette's revenge. Kittengarden must follow as sure as night follows day."

I stared out over the idyllic scene. HA doing so well, learning so fast, looking so good – good enough already to get gasps of admiration from those Otherside snickwitterers. She saw me watching and waved,

"Aren't I fantabulous!"

'Glidia' waved too, making a wide circle round the rink on her blades. "She is. I'm very proud of her!"

As she passed close to the Dragon – making us all jump – he SNARLED.

"See what I mean, RB," said Grimey. "The Dragon knows."

Dawn Of The Day Of The Third Night Of Grave Dancing

Dear Diary,

After Grimey had gone, HA and 'Glidia' came off the ice.

Now I was looking,
I could see something sly
in Glidia's face.

And there was something pointed and testing in the way she said it was time to go home and get ready for the Second Night of Waking the Dead.

HA, of course, thinking she was talking to a friend, went off like a Hags' Firework party:

"Dancing on Graves? Waking dead Othersiders? In the hope they'll drag themselves up and waft about as shades of their former selves for our entertainment? Really, those ossified old High Hags with their doddified ideas of FUN, need to get a grip on their broomsticks! So I don't have to go and get ready, Glidia – because I'm not going."

Well, if Glidia/Froggspittal was slyly trying to get HA to condemn herself she'd got more than she bargained for. She had to turn away to hide how choking she was at HA's insults to Hags.

When she turned back, I could really see Froggspittal in the cruel glitter of her eyes as she changed the subject and said, "You know, Hagatha, it seems a waste to be up here and not get some Dragon's Tears. Such a precious ingredient of spells. And never easy to come by. So send your Familiar over to make that beast cry, there's a dear. Oh...and here's a jar to collect the tears in."

HA stuttered a shocked protest – and did not take the jar.

At the same moment, as if he'd heard, the Dragon was loping across the ice, eyes as red as hot coals, nostrils snorting fire – making straight for Glidia/Froggspittal.

I yelled, "Look out! Behind you!" (whoever she was, I had to warn her) as from above us a voice called, "Easy! I've got him!" AND THERE, CIRCLING ABOVE THE DRAGON, WAS A FAMILIAR

I, for one, was certainly not familiar with.

A Familiar I'd never seen before.

She pulled a sprinkling vial from her pocket and...using the same spell as I'd used to freeze over his bog...

she turned the Dragon to ICE!!

And when she'd done that terrible deed, as if it was nothing to her, she called, "Just passing!" and flew away.

A tad of tell later it began to dawn on me – the unfamiliar Familiar had to be Anchovette in disguise! It had to be! Because who else had that Freezing spell? No one – no one at all. Grimey and I had been the FIRST to break its seal in the library. Only he and I and...Anchovette's eavesdropper, of course, who would have passed it on to her, had ever set eyes on it let alone used!!

As the unfamiliar Familiar (Anchovette for sure) disappeared, Glida/Froggspittal cackled. "Well...that was lucky, wasn't it. A friendly passing Familiar. Pity about the tears, but at least now we don't have a Dragon to interfere with your SKATING progress, do we, Hagatha? Anyway, must dash. See you tomorrow for your next lesson!"

As she mounted her broomstick and took off, HA ran over to the Dragon.

"Oh you poor dear creature. Frozen to your last breath."

To me she said, "What was all that about, RB? What would that Familiar have been doing here? Nobody 'just passes' across the Narrow Avoid."

I sat her down by the fire and MADE her listen – telling her the whole story as Grimey had told it to me.

Still she wasn't convinced – or didn't want to be.

"But we don't know for CERTAIN she's really Froggspittal or that the passing Familiar was Anchovette!"

"We do," I said. "I'll tell you how." And I explained about the Freezing spell and how the Spell Book it was in had never been opened before we opened it and no one except me, Grimey – and Anchovette via her eavesdropper – knew of it.

"Well, maybe that Familiar went to the library after you and found it," HA pouted.

"Possibly," I said. "But why? Far more likely it was Anchovette. Anchovette who knew, through her eavesdropper, there'd be a fiery Dragon to contend with while her Hag gave you skating lessons – and who came up here armed with the spell in case of trouble with him. We're done for, HA. Grimey is right. We're skating on thin ice.

And it's **cracking**.

We're for the sulphurous bog – you struck off and me hairless and sent back to Awethunders' kittengarden."

She slumped for a while staring at the frozen Dragon.

Then she recovered her spirit – the great spirit of the witch she is when she wants to be.

"DONE FOR?" she snapped.

"We'll see about 'DONE FOR'!

But first things first, RB!"

She got up and put her arms round the Dragon.

"First we must unfreeze him."

"Not possible," I said.

"Not for three moons. That's the Small Print in the spell."

"Three moons!" she cried.

"Why, he'll not just be frozen by then, he'll be dead.

THINK OF SOMETHING, RB!

THINK!"

As it happened, her hugging him, as if trying to warm him, gave me the idea.

"What about this," I said. "The spell's Small Print says 'no known SPELL exists to reverse the freezing-over in less than three moons'. It doesn't say it can't be reversed

BY OTHER MEANS.

So why don't we try

WARMING him?"

Her face lit up. "Supernova thinking! Furthermore I'm sure there's nothing that says we can't use a spell to assist us in not using a spell. If you follow?"

I did – sort of. Though it didn't prepare me for what happened next.

Standing quite still, pointing her spelling finger at the Horizon Line, she chanted in a voice that rang out across the Narrow Avoid and far far beyond:

"Blankets and covers
and bright woolly hats,
Long coats and short coats
and warm-woven mats,
Eiderdowns, quilted or patchworked or frilled,
Fly to us now and help ward off the chill!
Candlewick bedspreads
and long flannel johns,
Cloaks lined with velvet
and gowns from school dons,
Winter pi-jimjams
just warmed by the fire,
Come make the temp'rature
rise a lot higher!"

And flapping and flying they came – all the WARMING MATERIALS you could imagine – from This Side and the Other Side for all I could tell – filling the evening sky and fluttering down around us like clouds of giant butterflies.

We worked together. Draping and piling them on, until every scrap of iced Dragon was covered under many layers.

To increase the heat, HA spelled our fire into thirteen copies of itself which – obedient to her orders – created a circle and directed their smoulder towards him.

"Now we wait," said HA.

"For melt down."

We huddled beside one of the fires and fell to silence, busy with our thoughts.

Mine turned, of course, to the second night of grave-dancing. To Claudine and her hopes of dancing with me. Sorry Claudine, I thought, it isn't going to be tonight. Or ever. If Anchovette gets her way.

I had just closed an eye – to snatch a nap and some tell out from worrying – when HA leapt up crying,

"IT'S BEGINNING!"

The warming materials, soaked with melting ice, had started to slip and slide. There were nostrils to be seen. An eye... and it blinked. More covers and coats slopped to the ground. A great foot moved, its wet claws shining in the moonlight.

HA ran round in circles of delight. "He's thawing RB! But he's going to need some inner warming too! And fast."

She pointed her spelling finger at the thirteen fires, produced thirteen cooking pots, and chanted:

"And this iced beast, lest his life end,
Needs some hot food – if he's to mend.
So now he's been warmed
by the covers and coats,
Make him a porridge of
magic and oats!"

By the time the Dragon had shucked off the remaining covers, stretched, touched his talons a few times and snorted a little fire of his own, the bowls of hot milk and oats were ready.

He ate hungrily and messily – licked the dishes – and said,

"Thanking you.
And now, we make lesson for
Tear-Stealers and
Me-Freezers."

"OH YES!" HA cried. "You see, RB, we're nowhere near trapped!"

With that she spelled all the WARMING MATERIALS dry and sent them back to where they came from and the thirteen fires back into one.

"To remove the evidence," she laughed. "Before we plan the lesson."

Tell you more later – just GOT to get some shut-eye before this giant day begins!

A Few Hours Before Third Night Of Grave Dancing Begins (And I'm Going!)

Dear Diary,

Well, dear Diary, we've given Froggspittal and Anchovette a lesson to remember all right – by the stink of it – if nothing else.

Where to begin? I'll start with the Dragon's frozen bog, this morning. I wasn't there yet, but he was – playing his part to perfection as we'd planned –

THINNING THE ICED-OVER BOG

WITH HIS NOW UNFROZEN

FIERY BREATH!!

By the time HA, myself and Glidia arrived for this afternoon's skating lesson, the ice was thin enough to crack if you so much as stepped on it.

Also, as planned, the Dragon had resumed the pose of his frozen self exactly where Glidia/Froggspittal had left him.

No doubt you can guess the rest??

"Now, before we begin the lesson," HA said to Glidia/Froggspittal, "please do perform something from the Glassindia Ice Show. Using the whole rink, to astound me with your skills and show me what I should aspire to."

Well, few of us can resist showing off our skills. And even though hers were acquired by spelling not hard work, 'Glidia' didn't hesitate.

HA and I stood beside the Dragon
– cheering inwardly –
AS SHE SPED OUT ONTO THE THIN ICE.

In a few tads of tell it was cracking beneath her!

In her panic, as she began to sink, Froggspittal completely forgot to stay 'being Glidia' and became what she was and is:

A TRICKSOME OLD HAG,
UP TO HER NECKLACES
IN SQUELCHY, SULPHUROUS
BOG
AND SCREECHING
FOR MERCY!!

Of course, 'That Passing Familiar' – Anchovette – now came screaming through the air to rescue her Hag, not even bothering to keep herself disguised!!

As she went, HA called, "And a little lesson for you, Anchovette. Jealousy and revenge always get us up to our necks in Deep Squelch and Big Stink in the end!"

I haven't yet heard HOW Anchovette rescued her, but however she did it, she got up to her whiskers in the bog too.

I know this because Grimey has just been round. Apparently, the sulphurous stench of the two of them is all over Wizton. It's so bad that Dame Amuletta has forbidden them to go anywhere near anything – especially the last night of Grave Dancing.

Not so me! HA has given me full permission to attend. In fact, she's given me her blessing.

So, dear Diary, in a few hours I'll be tripping the stones with the Enchanting One, no Anchovette – and her dangerous 'long line of future familiar' expectations – anywhere in sight!

Needless to say, HA is sticking to her beliefs and is NOT attending.

Instead, she's gone skating on the Other Side.

"I think I'm ready to show those Guffawers, RB," she said as she left. "Wipe the snickwitter off their faces. And another thing. I've decided to start a skating school for witches. So if anybody asks or points a pointing finger at you – THAT is why you froze the Dragon's bog and found me an Instructor. Well, I had to learn first!"

And I must say she IS so good on those knife blades, I can see it now...

Haggy Aggy and the Skating Witches of Dragon's Bog in their famous Narrow Avoid Ice Show.

Well, at least it'll keep her occupied here – on This Side, with us – where, when she's willing, she so wondrously belongs.

WITCHES' CHARTER
OF GOOD PRACTICE

1. Scare at least one child on the Other Side into his or her wits – every day (excellent), once in seven days (good), once a moon (average), once in two moons (bad), once in a blue moon (failed).

2. Identify any fully-grown Othersiders who were not properly scared into their wits as children and DO IT NOW. (It is never too late for a grown Othersider to come to his or her senses.)

3. Invent a new spell useful for every purpose and every occasion in the Witches' Calendar. Ensure you or your Familiar commits it to a Spell Book before it is lost to the Realms of Forgetfulness for ever.

4. Keep a proper witch's house at all times – filled with dust and spiders' webs, mould and earwigs underthings and ensure the jars on your kitchen shelves are always alive with good spell ingredients.

5. Cackle a lot. Cackling can be heard far and wide and serves many purposes such as (i) alerting others to your terrifying presence (ii) sounding hideous and thereby comforting to your fellow witches.

6. Make sure your Familiar keeps your means of proper travel (broomsticks) in good trim and that one, either or both of you exercise them regularly.

7. Never fail to present yourself anywhere and everywhere in full witch's uniform (i.e. black everything and no ribbons upon your hat ever). Sleeping in uniform is recommended as a means of saving dressing time.

8. Keep your Familiar happy with a good supply of Comfrey and Slime Buns. Remember, behind every great witch is a well-fed Familiar.

9. At all times acknowledge the authority of your local High Hags. As their eyes can do 360 degrees and they know everything there is to know, it is always in your interests to make their wishes your commands.

CONTRACT OF SERVICE

between
WITCH HAGATHA AGATHA, Haggy Aggy for short, HA for shortest
of Thirteen Chimneys, Wizton-under-Wold
&
the Witch's Familiar,
RUMBLEWICK SPELLWACKER MORTIMER B, RB for short

It is hereby agreed that, come
FIRE, Brimstone, CAULDRONS overflowing
or ALIEN WIZARDS invading,
for the NEXT SEVEN YEARS
RB will serve HA,
obey her EVERY WHIM AND WORD and at all times assist her
in the ways of being a true and proper WITCH.

PAYMENT for services will be:
* a log basket to sleep in * unlimited Slime Buns for breakfast
* free use of HA's broomsticks (outside of peak brooming hours)
* and a cracked mirror for luck.

PENALTY for failing in his duties will be decided on the whim of
THE HAGS ON HIGH.

SIGNED AND SEALED
this New Moon Day, 22nd of Remember

Haggy Aggy
....
Witch Hagatha Agatha

Rumblewick
....
Rumblewick Spellwacker Mortimer B

Trixie Fiddlestick
....
And witnessed by the High Hag, Trixie Fiddlestick

ORCHARD BOOKS

338 Euston Road, London NWI 3BH
Orchard Books Australia
Level I7/207 Kent Street, Sydney NSW 2000

ISBN: 978 I 846I6 068 4

First published in 2008 by Orchard Books

Text © Hiawyn Oram 2008
Cover illustrations © Sarah Warburton 2008
Inside illustrations © Orchard Books 2008

The rights of Hiawyn Oram to be identified as the author
has been asserted by her

in accordance with the Copyright,
Designs and Patents Act, I988.

A CIP catalogue record for this book is
available from the British Library.

Orchard Books is a division
of Hachette Children's Books

I 3 5 7 9 I0 8 6 4 2
Printed in China/Hong Kong

To NSG who saved me from thin ice
(more than once)
H.O.

For Ethan
S.W.

Dear Precious Children

The Publisher asked me to say something about these Diaries. (As I do not write Otherside very well, I have dictated it to the Publisher's Familiar/assistant. If she has not written it down right, let me know and I'll turn her into a fat pumpkin.)

This is my message: I went to a lot of trouble to steal these Diaries for you. And the Publisher gave me a lot of shoes in exchange. If you do not read them the Publisher may want the shoes back. So please, for my sake – the only witch in witchdom who isn't willing to scare you for her own entertainment – ENJOY THEM ALL.

Yours ever,

Haggy Aggy

Your fantabulous shoe-loving friend,

Hagatha Agatha (Haggy Aggy for short, HA for shortest) xx

ISBN 9781846160653
ISBN 9781846160691
ISBN 9781846160721
ISBN 9781846160714
ISBN 9781846160677
ISBN 9781846160660
ISBN 9781846160707
ISBN 9781846160684

Dragon's Bog
Dragon's Cave
The Narrow Avoid
BEYOND WIZTON
N
W
E
S
CRAFTY CO-OP
OTHERSIDE
WIZTON